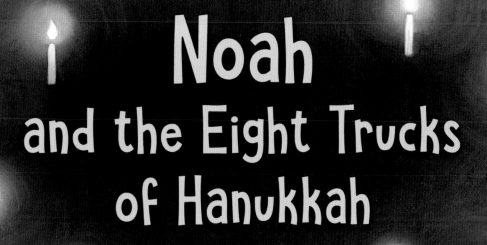

Noah
and the Eight Trucks
of Hanukkah

Nancy Rips

Illustrated by Marina Saumell

PELICAN PUBLISHING COMPANY
Gretna 2019

The word "Pelican" and the depiction of a pelican are
trademarks of Pelican Publishing Company, Inc., and are
registered in the U.S. Patent and Trademark Office.

Library of Congress Cataloging-in-Publication Data

Names: Rips, Nancy, author. | Saumell, Marina, illustrator.
Title: Noah and the eight trucks of Hanukkah / by Nancy Rips ; illustrated by
  Marina Saumell.
Description: Gretna : Pelican Publishing Company, 2018. | Summary: "Noah
  is a young boy who loves Hanukkah, but his favorite thing in the whole
  world is trucks. Why aren't they part of the Hanukkah celebration? In this
  story, Noah devises a way to have a Festival of Trucks along with the
  Festival of Lights, each honoring the brave Maccabees."—Provided by
  publisher.
Identifiers: LCCN 2016003404| ISBN 9781455622030 (hardcover : alk.
paper) | ISBN 9781455622047 (e-book)
Subjects: | CYAC: Hanukkah—Fiction. | Trucks—Fiction.
Classification: LCC PZ7.1.R5754 No 2018 | DDC [E]—dc23 LC record
available at https://lccn.loc.gov/2016003404

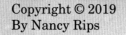

Printed in Malaysia
Published by Pelican Publishing Company, Inc.
1000 Burmaster Street, Gretna, Louisiana 70053
www.pelicanpub.com

To Doc, Noah's great-grandfather, with love—N. R.

Once there was a little boy named Noah. He had a mommy and a daddy and a big fluffy dog named Milo. Noah loved Hanukkah but his favorite thing in the whole world was trucks.

He loved shiny red fire trucks. He loved giant green garbage trucks.

He loved colorful ice cream trucks. And he really loved rumbling cement trucks.

The week before Hanukkah, Mommy began getting ready for the holiday. She took out the menorah, the big frying pan to make latkes, and all the colored dreidels.

Noah asked, "But where are the trucks?"

"Hanukkah isn't about trucks, Noah.
It's about the Jewish people and the brave
Maccabees. We call it the Festival of Lights.
We'll light a candle each night on the
menorah for eight nights," Mommy told him.

"I like candles but I like trucks better.
Could we have eight trucks of Hanukkah
this year?" Noah asked.

Mommy thought and thought. When Daddy came home they talked about it. "Trucks are strong. They go on all kinds of bumpy roads every day. Hanukkah is about Judah Maccabee and his brave soldiers. They were strong just like trucks. I think we could have eight trucks of Hanukkah this year!" Daddy said.

Noah was so happy. He went to sleep dreaming about trucks all night long.

On the first night of Hanukkah, Mommy, Daddy, and Noah lit the Shamash. Then they lit the first candle on the menorah and sang the blessings. Mommy beamed, "Noah, here's your present for tonight." Noah opened a box with a shiny red fire truck. He was so happy. He took it right up to his bedroom.

On the second night of Hanukkah they ate yummy latkes. Then Mommy called, "Look what Grandma and Grandpa sent from Chicago. It's a great green garbage truck!"

CHICAGO

Dear Noah,

Have a great Hanukkah!

Love,
Grandma and Grandpa

Noah clapped his hands in
glee and zoomed upstairs.

On the third night of Hanukkah they played dreidels. Then Noah opened a huge box from Uncle Tom. It was a toy cement truck with a card. "When you get older, I'll show you how real cement trucks help build strong buildings!" Uncle Tom wrote.

Noah,

When you get older,
I'll show you how real
cement trucks help build
strong buildings!

Your Uncle Tom

Noah ran the cement truck
straight to his bedroom.

On the fourth night of Hanukkah, Noah thought there couldn't be any more trucks. That was before Mommy let him open Aunt Wendy's present.

HAPPY HANUKKAH!

With love,
your Aunt Wendy

It was a dump truck! He jumped
up and down. Then he wheeled it
up the stairs to his room.

On the fifth night, Noah spied a
present from Nanny in New York.

NEW YORK

Dear Noah,

Hope to see you soon.
Happy Hanukkah!

Nanny

He couldn't believe it. She mailed him
a yellow bulldozer that looked so real!
He flew upstairs with it to his bedroom.

On the sixth night, Mommy showed him a package from Aunt Jane and Uncle Nate.

Noah,

Keep on trucking!
And have an amazing Hanukkah.

Aunt Jane
and
Uncle Nate

"It's a tow truck! I love tow trucks."
And up to his room he went with it.

On the seventh night, he opened a present
from his cousin Leo. All the way from Montana!

Greetings from

MONTANA

It was a silver tanker truck.
Noah drove it up to his bedroom.

On the last night of Hanukkah, Mommy and Daddy said to Noah, "You have one more present. It's from your favorite babysitter, Rachel."

It was an ice-cream truck. There were pictures of ice-cream treats all over the outside. Noah had a big smile on his face as he danced it upstairs to his room.

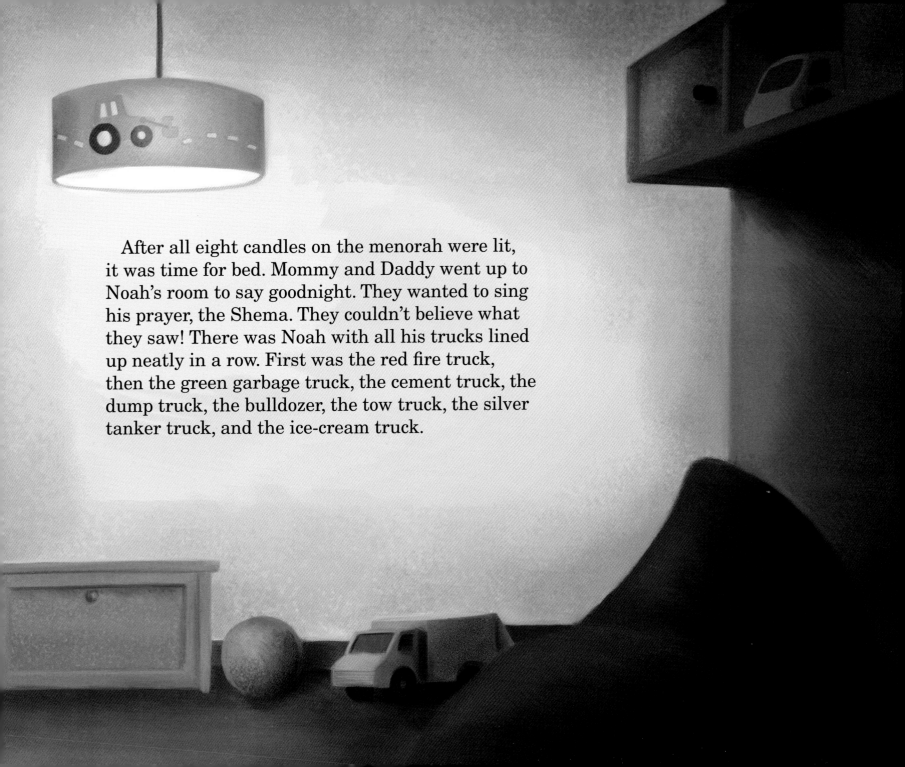

After all eight candles on the menorah were lit, it was time for bed. Mommy and Daddy went up to Noah's room to say goodnight. They wanted to sing his prayer, the Shema. They couldn't believe what they saw! There was Noah with all his trucks lined up neatly in a row. First was the red fire truck, then the green garbage truck, the cement truck, the dump truck, the bulldozer, the tow truck, the silver tanker truck, and the ice-cream truck.

"This is my play menorah. Each of the trucks is one night of Hanukkah and I'm the Shamash. I'm the strong leader of the group, just like Judah Maccabee! I tell each of them when it's their turn to light up and shine. We're having a Festival of Trucks *and* a Festival of Lights!" Noah jumped into bed. He was excited that he could honor the brave Maccabees with his eight trucks of Hanukkah.

AUTHOR'S NOTE

For a while, whenever I saw my grandson Noah, he had a toy truck in each hand. He brought them on walks and to the park, and he even splashed rolling, rubber models in the bathtub. At bedtime, he snuggled up under the covers with his favorites and listened to stories about trucks.

It made me wonder why there were no Jewish holiday books showing little boys and trucks. Many feature families celebrating together, but there was not one combining holidays with Noah's favorites: cement mixers, dump trucks, and fire trucks. That's how ***Noah and the Eight Trucks of Hanukkah*** came to be.

Noah's older now and prefers trains. Maybe they'll make an appearance with Noah in a book soon. All aboard!